This igloo book belongs to:

....

igloobooks

*Published in 2019
by Igloo Books Ltd
Cottage Farm
Sywell
NN6 0BJ
www.igloobooks.com*

Copyright © 2017 Igloo Books Ltd
Igloo Books is an imprint of Bonnier Books UK

*Illustrated by Jacqui Davis
Written by Stephanie Moss*

*Cover designed by Lee Italiano
Interiors designed by Jason Shortland
Edited by Hannah Cather*

1119 003
6 8 10 12 11 9 7 5
ISBN 978-1-78670-926-4

Printed and manufactured in China

Sparkly Fairy Stories

igloobooks

Fairy
Crystabelle's
New Dress

Fairy Crystabelle couldn't wait to go to the magical Fairyland Ball,
but when she looked inside her wardrobe, she had nothing to wear at all.

"What am I going to do?" poor Fairy Crystabelle cried.
She'd never have time to make a new dress, however hard she tried.

"Don't worry," said her friends. "Everything will be fine.
We can make you a ballgown that is sure to shimmer and shine."

So they **fluttered** their fairy wings and went into the fairy wood, to find as many things for her new dress as they **possibly** could.

They found **toadstools,** leaves and petals lying on the ground.
They took out their magic wands and **swished** them all around.

Crystabelle's new dress looked **better** than she could have dreamed.
It shimmered with fairy dust and jewels that **glittered** and gleamed.

When Crystabelle arrived at the ball, everyone began to stare.
All her fairy friends thought she was the **prettiest** fairy there.

"I'm so pleased," said Crystabelle, "that we made my dress together."
Then she twirled around and said, "You are the best friends ever!"

Fairy
Sparklepop's
Big Moment

Fairy Sparklepop dreamed of being a **star,** so she could sing and dance.
When Fairyland held a talent contest, she finally got her chance.

"Why don't we start a pop band?" suggested Fairy Twinkletoes. "We'll have so much fun together and wear sparkly pop-star clothes."

They cast a **spell** for a guitar and a tinkly keyboard, too.
They turned toadstools into **drums** and used their wands to sing into.

As soon as they were ready, they set up a stage in the **fairy** wood.
They rehearsed together **all** day long, as often as they could.

On the day of the contest, the fairies were the **stars** of the show.
They sang the very best pop songs and they danced around to and fro.

"We love the fairy pop stars!" cheered the crowd, loudly, to the band.
So it was no surprise when they won the contest, for being the **best** in Fairyland.

Fairy
Twinkletoes'
Dancing Feet

The fairies were excited for the **disco** in Fairyland,
but why they were so **happy,** one fairy couldn't understand.

Fairyland
Disco

Twinkletoes wasn't excited. She knew her dancing was really bad.
So she sat down on a toadstool, feeling **nervous** and quite sad.

"You just need to be brave," Fairy Crystabelle would say.
"We'll show you what to do, so you're ready on the day."

The fairies turned on the
music and **danced**
along to the beat.

They showed Twinkletoes how to **twirl** and **tap** her little feet.

On the night of the **disco,** Twinkletoes still wasn't prepared.
"Don't worry," said her friends. "There's no need to be scared!"

The fairies set off to the disco at **Sparkle Lake.**
They reassured their friend she wouldn't make a mistake.

When they got to the disco, everything **twinkled** with fairy light.
Suddenly, Fairy Twinkletoes couldn't wait to dance **all** night!

The little fairy danced and pranced. She swirled and **twirled.**
Twinkletoes could really move and it was the **best** feeling in the world.